PARKING PANDEMONIUM

A

FABLES FROM THE LETTER PEOPLE

BOOK

WRITTEN BY:

ELAYNE REISS-WEIMANN

RITA FRIEDMAN

ILLUSTRATED BY:

ELIZABETH CALLEN

NEW DIMENSIONS IN EDUCATION
Division of Abrams & Company Publishers, Inc.
61 MATTATUCK HEIGHTS
WATERBURY, CT 06705

Printed in U.S.A.

ISBN 0-89796-015-7

3 4 5 6 7 8 9   SPC   0 9 8 7 6 5   013301P

In Letter People Land, very few people drive cars.

Most people prefer to walk or ride bicycles.

Mr. P rides his pony.

But every weekend, people come from everywhere

to visit Letter People Land.

They come in cars.

Then parking becomes a problem.

The problem starts when Mr. P and his pointy patches
plan a picture book parade for Saturday afternoon.
''Children can dress as their favorite story book
friends,'' says the librarian.
''We'll start at the library, parade down Main Street
into the park and past the pond,'' says Mr. P.
''We can have a party and play in the park's picnic
area,'' say the pointy patches.
''A picture book parade and a party in the park!
We are planning a pleasant day,'' says Mr. P.

Soon it is Saturday, the day of the parade.

"It is time to meet the children at the library,"

says Mr. P.

Polka Dot Patch steps out onto the porch.

"Mr. P, cars are parked everywhere," she cries.

"There are cars parked on our lawn.

There are cars parked on our neighbors' lawns too."

"Cars are parked zig zag, sideways, this way

and that way," says Purple Patch, peeking outside.

"There is parking pandemonium," says Mr. P.

"People shouldn't park their cars anywhere they please."

"I'll have to squeeze between the cars," says Mr. P.
"We'll pop from car to car," say the pointy patches.
"Give us your hand, Mr. P, and we'll pull you."
Finally, after squeezing, pulling, and popping,
the pointy patches and Mr. P get to Main Street.
"Look!" says Pink Patch.
"Cars are parked all over the road."
"People should not park anyplace they please.
We planned the parade.
Someone has to plan parking," says Mr. P.

MAIN ST.

The children wait patiently at the library for Mr. P
and the pointy patches.
"We cannot have our parade," say the children.
"Cars are parked where we are planning to parade."
"The parked cars will have to be moved," says Mr. P.
"We could push the cars," say the pointy patches.
"No," says Mr. P, "we shouldn't move other people's
property without their permission.
We'll use loudspeakers and call the people back
to the cars."

MAIN ST.

People hear the loudspeakers.
They hurry to their parked cars.
"We didn't know where to park and where not to park,"
the people say.
Finally, after one hour, all the cars are moved.
The children parade down Main Street into the park,
past the pond, and to the park's picnic area.
The parade and the party are great fun.
"Things work out well when you plan," says Mr. P.

The next day, Mr. P thinks about the parking problem.
He goes out to his garden to pick some petunias.
He looks at the rows and rows of plants.
"I planned my garden so each plant has a place to grow.
Parking should be planned so each car has a place
to park," thinks Mr. P.
Mr. P calls the pointy patches.
"We need to plan for parking," says Mr. P.
"We can make parking places
by painting lines on the street."

Mr. P and the pointy patches carry pails of paint
and paint brushes out onto Main Street.
Mr. P looks up and down Main Street.
"Where shall we paint the parking places?"
ask the pointy patches.
"Let's paint yellow lines on the street," says Mr. P.
"Each car can park between two yellow lines.
I'll go get a ruler to measure the parking places."
Mr. P rushes back to his house.
While Mr. P is gone, the pointy patches start painting.

Mr. P runs back to Main Street.

"Please stop painting," pleads Mr. P.

"These parking places won't work.

Some lines are painted too close together.

These parking places are too small.

Some lines are painted too far apart.

These parking places are too big.

You cannot paint lines anywhere you please.

To have planned parking, you need

planned parking places."

Mr. P uses his ruler to plan the parking places.
Mr. P measures the parking places to be sure
they are the right size.
The pointy patches paint and paint.
Soon there are parking places all along Main Street.
"How will people know we have painted parking places?"
ask the pointy patches.
"We can print the words 'PARKING PLACE'
in each space," says Pink Patch.
"That's a perfect plan," smiles Mr. P.

The next Saturday, Mr. P and the pointy patches
help a police officer direct traffic on Main Street.
The drivers are pleased to have places to park.
"Mr. P, I think our parking plan is working,"
says Purple Patch.
"We may still have problems," says Mr. P.
"There are more cars than parking places."
The parking places fill very quickly.
Then parking pandemonium starts again.

People drive up and down Main Street
looking for a parking place.
But the parked cars stay parked.
After a long time, people are not patient anymore.
They toot their horns.
The noise gets louder and louder.
"This is not a good parking plan," they protest.
"We have no place to park.
The parked cars stay parked for hours and hours."

"Mr. P, what shall we do?" asks Polka Dot Patch.
"People say our parking plan is not good."
"Our parking plan is good," says Mr. P.
"But we have to add more to our plan.
We have to make sure people share the parking places.
Next Saturday, parked cars will not stay parked
for more than one hour."

All week, Mr. P and the pointy patches print signs.

They attach the signs to posts.

They put a post on the sidewalk by each parking place.

Then one pointy patch pops on top of each sign.

"Remember what the printed signs say," says Mr. P.

" 'Parking—One hour limit! Pay 25¢.'

You collect the money and give it to the mayor."

This time, planned parking works.

No one has to wait a long time for a parking place.

25¢
PARKING
One Hour Limit!
PAY 25¢

People ask Mr. P to put parking places
on other busy streets.
Then there are not enough pointy patches
to be in every parking place to collect money.
"We have to add to the parking plan again," says Mr. P.
"Instead of pointy patches, we'll use parking meters
to collect money for parking places."
"Mr. P, what will our job be?" ask the pointy patches.
"You'll check the meters," says Mr. P.

29

Now people put money in parking meters.
If they forget to return to their cars after one hour
they find a pointy patch waiting for them.
''Please be considerate of other people who want
to park,'' says the pointy patch politely.
Most people never need to be reminded more than once.